COLLECTING SMILES

OUT NOW!

BUBBLES

written and illustrated by huy truong

DREAMS

COMING IN MAY 2011

COLLECTING HUGS

COMING IN MAY 2011

COLLECTING GIFTS

COMING IN SEPT 2011

ADVENTURES

COMING IN SEPT 2011

DIMENSIONAL ENTERTAINMENT RARA

WWW.PWANDA.CO.UK

Playtime with... PWANDA!™

Series

For Sam.

COLLECTING BUBBLES
Written and Illustrated by Huy Truong.

Based on characters originally created by Dil.

Writing and Illustrations - Huy Truong. BA (Hons), PGCE.
Producer - Dil.
Original Character Design - Phil Knott. BA (Hons).
Editor - Dips.

Director of Operations - Subodh Dhanda. BSc (Hons), M Res.
C.E.O/Director of Marketing - Dil
Special Thanks to Neil Turner, Vinod Dhanda and Svati Khajuria.

Published by Dimensional Entertainment
PO BOX 5087
Wolverhampton
WV1 9GY
United Kingdom, England
Visit our website at
WWW.PWANDA.CO.UK
WWW.DIMENSIONALONLINE.COM

First print, 2010.

ISBN 978-0-9556274-2-2

Printed in India.

WWW.PWANDA.CO.UK

BUBBLES

Written and Illustrated
by Huy Truong

DIMENSIONAL ENTERTAINMENT RARA

WWW.PWANDA.CO.UK

The sun has been burning oh so bright,
And there is not a cloud at all in sight.

It's been getting hotter
and hotter,

And the village has
run out of water.

Dipsyfear the Pwanda bear is trying to think,
Where he can find some water to drink.

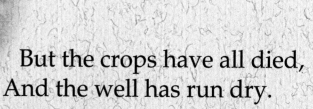

But the crops have all died,
And the well has run dry.

The well is empty and hollow,
And all he finds is a thirsty echo.

There is no water to drink anywhere,
The water that's left is not being shared.

The little Pwanda
decides to take,

The long long journey
towards the lake.

Through the forest
and far away,

He sets off
down the lane
one day.

Eventually he finds the lake at last,
He drinks and drinks and drinks so fast.

He drinks until he's had his fill,
But then remembered what he faces still.

All the way back home he goes,
To tell the others what he knows.

So off they head with buckets and pails,
To fetch the water along the trail.

Dipsyfear gets really tired
and needs to rest his feet,

This fetching and carrying wate
has really got him beat.

They are all so tired
and they all agree,

That a much better way
there has to be.

What can they do? They do not know,
So Dipsyfear goes to see Dipillow.

He knows his Pwanda bear friend,
  Will have a helpful hand to lend.

Dipillow told him he was in a bubble,
And this made him feel quite muddled.

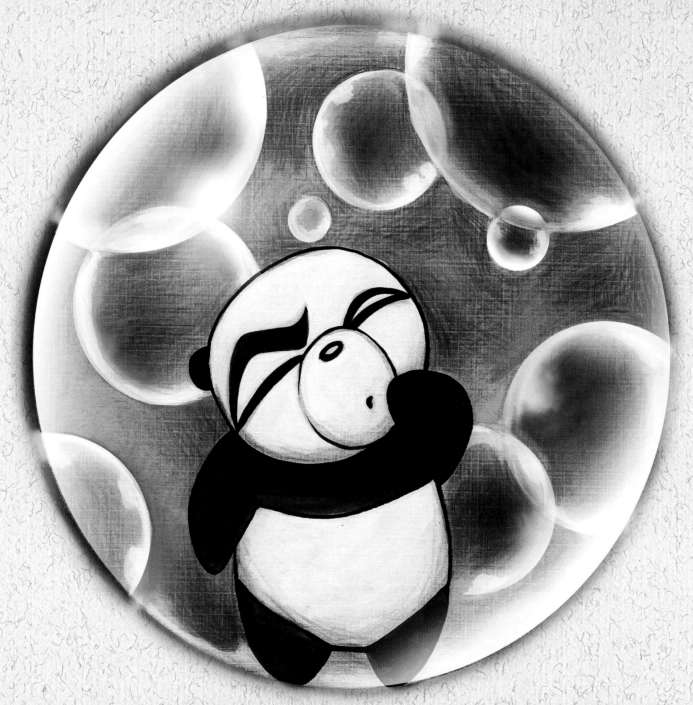

But he listened to what Dipillow said,
And occasionally nodded his head.

When you're all alone,
your problems seem much bigger.

When you're on your own,
It all seems much trickier.

What you need is a helping hand,
So your problem can be shared.

Someone to be a good friend,
To show you that they care.

Our bubbles keep us all apart,
So just reach out there for a start.

And join bubbles with one another,
You'll achieve so much more together.

So Dipsyfear all by himself,
Tries to join bubbles with someone else.

One and one makes two,
There's now twice as much that you can do.

You will always halve your troubles,
If you double all your bubbles.

Two and two makes four,
ow you can do twice as much as before.

You'll always halve your troubles,
When you double all your bubbles.

Four and four makes eight, which means
That eight and eight makes sixteen.

So their bubbles continue to double,
And each time they halve their troubles.

The crops in the fields still needed water to grow,
So they built a canal for the water to flow.

It works! It really is much better,
If you join and work together.

So soon the village has water again,
But now they have much more, it's plain.

By joining their bubbles, what they've really done,
Is manage to create a great big one.

This bubble continues to grow and grow,
There's absolutely no stopping it now.

Because you'll always halve your troubles,
If you double all your bubbles!

ABOUT THE AUTHOR

Huy Truong is an illustrator living in Somerset, England. He was born in 1972 in Saigon, Vietnam during the conflict. At the age of 7, he escaped with his family and fled his home country seeking refuge, eventually arriving in Great Britain.

Huy has had a passion for drawing since childhood and it was inevitable that his career would be founded on his talents. This led him to attain a degree in Industrial Design (BA Hons) from Cardiff University. Discovering he had a love of teaching also, he subsequently completed his Art Teaching certificate (PGCE) at Southampton University. This paved the way for a career teaching Art and becoming an examiner for EDEXCEL.

Besides teaching Art, Huy also taught Graphics, Textiles, Photography and Media Studies. He developed a passion for theatre Design by engaging in numerous productions in school and local theatres working as a Stage Designer, set painter and props maker. This led him to write, direct and stage his own play for a Youth Theatre Project funded by the local Council in Somerset. The project was aimed at developing Creative Arts for children of all backgrounds and giving them an opportunity to engage with the wider community. In addition, Huy ran a variety of Art and Craft workshops during the school holidays, teaching children a wide range of artistic disciplines.

Huy taught art for 12 years and after inspiring hoards of young creators decided to refocus on his own artwork. Currently, he is a freelance illustrator and a portraitist with his first range of 'Playtime with Pwanda!' children's books, written and illustrated for his daughters Grace and Emily.

PLAYTIME WITH PWANDA MERCHANDISE

"*Pwanda* is ready to take on the world. Go *Pwanda*!"

Richard Taylor (Weta Workshop – The Chronicles of Narnia, Avatar, his very own children's TV series The WotWots)

With huge support for Pwanda, Dimensional Entertainment is producing a TV animation programme based on *Playtime with Pwanda* children's books. The series is aimed at pre-school children and is designed to encourage the use of their imaginations and explore the realm of 'play'.

In addition to the Playtime with *Pwanda* children's book series The *Pwanda* brand now includes a *Pwanda! RaRa Dipsyfear* soft toy. This will be manufactured and distributed by global leaders **Aurora Worldwide** (www.auroraworld.com) who are also license holders of soft toys for *The Pink Panther* and *The Gruffalo*.

A fully comprehensive range of children's clothes featuring Dimensional Entertainment's *RaRa Dipsyfear* character have been released in mid 2010 by **The Garment Company** (www.thegarmentcompany.co.uk). Boys' and Girls' clothing and accessories for ages 3-13 years.

Finally, also available are children's wallpaper murals featuring the *Playtime with Pwanda* designs manufactured and distributed by **Atlas Wallcoverings BV** (www.atlaswallco.com). These are available though retail stores S.J Dixon and Brewster in the UK and USA respectively.

WWW.PWANDA.CO.UK

COLLECTING SMILES

OUT NOW!

BUBBLES

written and illustrated by huy truong

DREAMS

COMING IN MAY 2011

COLLECTING HUGS

COMING IN MAY 2011

COLLECTING GIFTS

COMING IN SEPT 2011

ADVENTURES

COMING IN SEPT 2011

DIMENSIONAL ENTERTAINMENT RA RA

WWW.PWANDA.CO.UK

Playtime with... PWANDA! Series